D0096057

# ZIBBY PAYNE

## & THE DRAMA TRAUMA

Published by Lobster Press™
1620 Sherbrooke Street West, Suites C & D
Montréal, Québec   H3H 1C9
Tel. (514) 904-1100 • Fax (514) 904-1101 • www.lobsterpress.com

Publisher: Alison Fripp
Editors: Alison Fripp & Meghan Nolan
Editorial Assistant: Katie Scott
Graphic Design & Production: Tammy Desnoyers


Library and Archives Canada Cataloguing in Publication

Bell, Alison
       Zibby Payne & the drama trauma / Alison Bell.

(Zibby Payne)
ISBN-13: 978-1-897073-47-6
ISBN-10: 1-897073-47-X

       I. Title.  II. Title: Zibby Payne and the drama trauma.
III. Series: Bell, Alison.  Zibby Payne

PZ7.B41528Zi 2007            j813'.6            C2006-903926-7

Printed and bound in Canada.

*To brainstormer extraordinaire, Karle Dickerson*
*And to my inspiration, Libby*

– Alison Bell

# ZIBBY PAYNE

## & THE DRAMA TRAUMA

written by

### Alison Bell

Lobster Press™

# CHAPTER 1

## THE PLAY'S NOT THE THING

"Go, Zibby, go!" Zibby's teammates yelled. Zibby Payne raced down the soccer field with the ball at her feet. Her class was playing Room 7 during morning recess, and the score was tied. As Zibby neared her team's goal, she drew her foot back and kicked the ball as hard as she could. The ball arched over the defenders and landed in the left-hand corner of the net.

"Goal!" yelled her teammate Matthew, throwing his arms up in the air. Her team won 3 - 2!

Zibby clasped her hands above her head in victory as the boys jogged over to congratulate her.

"Way to go," said Matthew, giving Zibby a high five.

"Thanks!" said Zibby.

Just then, the warning bell rang, signaling that recess was over and class would start in five minutes. Zibby said goodbye to the boys and ran off the field happy, sweaty, and with a streak of dirt above her left eyebrow. She played soccer with the boys almost every recess – when she wasn't hanging out with her best friend, Sarah, that is. Zibby loved the game, especially when she kicked in the game-winning goal!

Zibby walked over to the lunch tables next to the school library, sat down, and changed her shoes. She and Sarah wore one of each other's shoes almost every day, but playing soccer in mismatched footwear wasn't easy, especially since Sarah liked platforms and slip-ons – definitely not the best to run in. So Zibby brought soccer cleats to change into for recess. Now she put back on her green high-top sneaker and one of Sarah's light blue ballet flats.

As she stood up from the table, she noticed a small crowd of kids, including Sarah, gathering in front of the library door where teachers posted notices. Zibby slung her soccer cleats over her shoulder and hurried to join Sarah.

"What's up?" Zibby asked.

Sarah reached out and rubbed the smudge off Zibby's forehead before answering. "Mrs. Halpin just put up a flyer about the sixth-grade play," she said. "Auditions are tomorrow. I'm so excited!"

"Hmm," murmured Zibby with a little frown, not even bothering to look at the flyer. She'd been hoping the notice was about Something Interesting And Important, like a school soccer tournament. Not something as wimpy as the sixth-grade musical that the drama teacher, Mrs. Halpin, put on each year. Zibby wasn't an actress; she was a tomboy. And the last thing she ever wanted to do was put on some frilly costume and thick, sticky stage makeup.

But not Sarah. She'd been looking forward to the sixth-grade play since she was in kindergarten.

"Listen to this," she exclaimed. "Mrs. Halpin has written her own play this year. It's called *A Season of Change*, and it's about how an eleven-year-old girl named Miranda moves to a new school and finds more success than she ever could have dreamed. Cool plot!" she said, and turned to look at Zibby.

"Sounds fun," said Zibby. And she meant it. For Sarah, that is. Not for her.

Suddenly, Zibby was gently bumped from behind. She whirled around and there stood her friends – or more accurately, her "sort-of friends" – Amber and Camille. Lately, Zibby had grown apart from them because all they ever wanted to talk about was boys, lip gloss, and 101 ways to fix their hair – the exact three things Zibby did *not* want to talk about.

"What's this?" asked Amber, giving Sarah and Zibby a slight shove until she was planted right in front of the announcement with Camille in tow. She quickly read the notice, then cooed, "I *luv* the name Miranda. I hope I get the part. I really want to be the lead!" Amber looked around. "So is anyone else trying out?"

"I am," said Sarah. "I'd like to get a small, but interesting, role."

"I'm trying out, too," said Camille. "I'll be happy with anything I get – I just want to be part of the show."

"What about you, Zibby?" Amber took out a stick of

Groovy Grapilicious lip gloss from the pocket of her little jean skirt and applied some to her lips.

"Nope," Zibby shook her head. "I'll leave the acting to you guys."

"Less competition for me, then," Amber said cheerfully.

Zibby looked around and noticed most of the other kids were headed back to class. She didn't want to get her first late slip because of a play she wasn't even going to be in.

"We'd better move it," Zibby said. "Class is starting any minute." The four girls sprinted to their room just as their teacher, Miss Cannon, was closing the door.

* * *

After school that day, as Zibby and Sarah lingered by the lunch tables before walking home, Sarah tried to persuade Zibby to change her mind about the musical.

"Are you sure you won't try out with me?" she asked Zibby. "It would be a lot more fun if we were in the play together."

"Sorry," said Zibby. "You know I'm into soccer, not drama."

"But you might like it more than you think!" Sarah persisted.

For a moment, Zibby had a vision of herself standing in front of a clapping, adoring audience that was showering her with flowers as she gave bow after bow. And she had to admit, the image looked pretty good. But then she snapped back to reality. *Drama is for sissies, not for tomboys*, she reminded herself.

"Me being in a play would be like putting ketchup on ice cream," Zibby said. "Or chocolate sauce on a burger."

"Gross," Sarah said as she wrinkled up her nose.

"See?" said Zibby. "It just doesn't work!"

The two girls started to walk out of the school gate when they were joined by Amber and Camille, who were also chatting about the play.

"I hope no loser guys try out," Amber was saying. "Please let there be tons of cuties in the musical!"

Zibby rolled her eyes. *Are boys all Amber can ever think about?* she wondered.

"I can't wait to get my own script – with my name on it!" said Sarah, jumping into the conversation.

"I'm looking forward to my entire family seeing me on stage," said Camille, looking dreamily into the distance.

"And think how much fun the cast party will be!" added Sarah.

"Oh my gosh!" Amber squealed, grabbing Sarah and Camille both by an arm and pulling them toward her. "This play is going to be the most incredible experience – the high point of our entire sixth-grade year!"

"It sure is!" exclaimed Sarah.

"You know it!" said Camille.

The three girls burst into giggles, then began skipping down the street.

"Hey, wait for me!" called Zibby, hurrying to catch up with her friends and suddenly – and unexpectedly – feeling very left out.

# CHAPTER 2

## A STAR IS BORN

The next day as Zibby was sitting at the lunch table finishing her tuna fish sandwich, Amber slid in next to her.

"S-O-S!" cried Amber.

"What?" asked Zibby through a mouthful.

"I need your help!" she said.

"Really?" asked Zibby, crumpling up her sandwich wrapper. *What could Amber possibly want from me,* she wondered. *I don't have any lip gloss or styling gel to lend her.*

"I need you to teach me some soccer kicks," said Amber. "For the play."

"What do soccer kicks have to do with the play?" asked Zibby, perplexed.

"I was talking to Mrs. Halpin this morning, and she told me that the main character, Miranda, is a soccer player," Amber explained. "In fact, during the play, Miranda actually scores the winning goal that clinches the national championship for her team. And since I'm going to be Miranda, I need to know how to play soccer."

"But wait," Zibby said, even more confused. "The auditions haven't been held yet, have they?"

"No, but ..." Amber looked around as if to make sure no one was listening, then leaned in closer to Zibby. "I don't want to brag, but there's not much competition. I can sing, I can act, I can dance, and my parents say I could be the next Britney Spears," she flipped her shiny, straight blond locks over her shoulder. "I *know* Mrs. Halpin is going to choose me to be Miranda. So to be really authentic, I need to learn how to play soccer."

"Hmm," Zibby said, not sure if she should help Amber. It was irritating how Amber just assumed she was going to get the part of Miranda. Plus, as far as Zibby knew, Amber had never even touched a soccer ball, and being the one to teach her the sport didn't exactly sound like fun.

On the other hand, it might feel good to show off her soccer skills to Amber. Amber was always giving her grief for being a tomboy, so maybe now she'd finally show some respect to Zibby.

"Okay," said Zibby. "I'll do it."

"Right now?" asked Amber.

"I guess so," said Zibby. She'd been hoping to join the boys for some soccer, but she figured she could always play during afternoon recess instead.

"Thank you!" cried Amber, giving Zibby a little hug.

"Hey, what's that smell?" Zibby said as she sniffed the air when Amber released her.

"Do you like it?" asked Amber. "It's my new 'Fresh & Delightful Fragrance Stick' – a zingy blend of citrus fruits with a subtle hint of vanilla."

"Smells like the perfume department at Macy's," said Zibby, crinkling her nose. "Once when I was walking through the store with my mom, a lady working there spritzed me with something, and I stunk like rotten fruit for a week."

Amber's eyes narrowed. "I do not stink," she said crossly. Then she stood up. "Can we get going?" she asked impatiently.

"No prob," said Zibby, holding her breath to block her sense of smell in case anything else that was 'Fresh & Delightful' wafted her way.

The two girls walked out to a grassy area of the playground next to the soccer field where the PE teacher left a portable container of sporting equipment. Zibby dug into it and pulled out a soccer ball. It was flat – like most of the school balls, which were totally thrashed – but it would work well enough. She then placed the ball on the inside of Amber's right foot.

"Wait a minute," she said, pointing to Amber's plum-covered ballerina flats. "You sure you want to play in those shoes? You might get hurt – they don't give you much protection."

"I'll be fine," Amber said, and shook her head as if Zibby were bringing up the dumbest point anyone had ever made. "So what do I do?"

"Kick the ball using the inside of your foot," she explained. "This is called a push pass." Zibby backed away a few feet, and then said, "Now kick the ball to me."

Amber tentatively nudged the ball and it only rolled a few inches.

"Harder," commanded Zibby, retrieving the ball and putting it back beside Amber's foot.

"Okay," said Amber, sounding irritated, and she gave the ball a powerful *thwack* with her foot – so powerful, in fact, that the ball sailed way past Zibby a good twenty feet.

"Great kick," said Zibby, turning to admire how far the ball rolled. "Next time, though, a little softer so the ball comes to me."

Zibby was so distracted by the kick that she hadn't even noticed that Amber wasn't listening to her. She'd collapsed on the grass, screaming, "My toe, my big toe! It really hurts!" She ripped off her shoe and examined her bare foot. "And look!" she shrieked. "My nail polish is wrecked!"

She pointed at her big toenail, which, like the rest of her toes, was painted bright pink. Zibby bent down to study it, and indeed, she could detect a tiny chip near the top where the polish had come off.

"A tragedy," said Zibby, rolling her eyes.

"I *know*," Amber said earnestly. "I just had my nails done yesterday! And look," she screamed again. "My pinky toe's chipped too. I need an emergency pedicure!"

She reached into her skirt pocket and pulled out her tiny cell phone. "I just hope Camille has some of that 'Red Hot Pink' left," she said, speed-dialing Camille's number.

"Good luck," Zibby called out, leaving Amber sprawled on the field as she walked back to the lunch tables, dribbling the ball between her feet.

*She is so lame*, thought Zibby. *There's no way she'll ever be able to fake being a soccer player. Too bad someone who actually knows something about the sport isn't trying out to be Miranda. Someone who has talent and ability. Someone who deserves the role.*

And just then, Zibby quit dribbling the ball because she was hit with a Very Good Idea. *She* should try out for Miranda! Forget yesterday's idea about drama being only for wimps, because this was one role that for sure wasn't wimpy. Who better to play a soccer player than a *real* soccer player?

Plus, if she got into the play, she'd make Sarah happy *and* they'd get to spend tons of time together at rehearsals. And she did love to be the star on the field ... so why not on the stage?

The idea was seeming more brilliant by the millisecond, when someone tapped her on the shoulder. She turned around and saw that it was Matthew.

"How come you're not out there?" he asked, motioning over to the soccer field where the boys were playing.

"The sixth-grade musical is about a soccer player, and since Amber thinks she's getting the lead role, she wanted me to give her some pointers on how to play," she explained.

"Oh," said Matthew, sounding interested. "I wonder if any boys play soccer in the play because I'm trying out too."

Zibby's jaw dropped. "You are?" Matthew was a super jock, so she would never have dreamed he'd try out.

"My uncle's an actor," he said. "And my mom was a theater major in college. My family's really into drama."

"I'm trying out too!" she exclaimed. "I just made up my mind before you walked over."

Matthew grinned. "Hey, that's great. I'm glad I'll have one of my soccer buddies with me – most of the boys think acting's stupid."

"They're the ones who are stupid!" yelled Zibby. No one talked about the sixth-grade musical that way! Well, maybe she had yesterday, but now that she'd decided to try out, she'd turned into the play's Number One Fan.

Matthew glanced back at the game. "I'd better get going. See you at the audition, tomboy," he said, calling her by the special nickname only he used for her, and jogged back to the other boys.

Zibby picked up the ball, put it back in the equipment box, and ran over to the lunch benches, looking for Sarah so she could tell her the Big News. But just then, she remembered one tiny detail she'd failed to think about: She didn't have a clue about singing or acting! She'd never been in a show in her life ... unless the time she played a green pea in the preschool Thanksgiving feast pageant counted, and she doubted it did.

She stopped running and nervously rubbed her chin.

Did she even have a chance to make the musical? And even more pressing, what would the auditions be like?

# CHAPTER 3

## A VERY HAPPY BIRTHDAY TO YOU

Zibby quickly found Sarah sitting at the lunch table reading the latest Harry Potter book and crashed down on the bench across from her.

"Guess what?" Zibby asked eagerly. "I'm trying out for the play!"

"No way!" said Sarah, closing her book.

"Yes, way!" said Zibby. "Turns out Miranda is a soccer player, and I think I'd be perfect for the part. So I'm gonna do the play with you."

"That's great!" exclaimed Sarah. "I can't believe it!"

"But," continued Zibby, wrinkling her forehead, "Amber thinks she's getting the lead role – she says she's the next Britney Spears or something – so I may not have much of a chance. And I don't even know what auditions are like. Do you know what you have to do?"

"Don't worry about Amber – her head's pretty swollen lately, so she may think she's actually better than she is," said Sarah. "And for auditions, all you have to do is sing 'Happy Birthday.'"

"That's it?" asked Zibby.

"Mrs. Halpin's been doing this for a long time, and

she says she can tell everything about someone's acting and singing abilities just by how well they sing 'Happy Birthday,'" said Sarah.

Zibby felt relieved. "I think I can do that – I mean, I've sung it at a zillion birthday parties."

"Of course you can," said Sarah supportively. "Just practice the song a few times at home, and you'll be all set."

* * *

"The actress has arrived," Zibby yelled as she walked through her front door that afternoon.

"What?" her mom called from the kitchen.

"I'm auditioning for the sixth-grade musical," announced Zibby, storming into the kitchen where her mom and three-year-old brother, Sam, were baking cookies. She swiped a few freshly baked double chocolate chip cookies off the plate. "I'm trying out for the lead girl – it's really cool because she's a soccer player."

"I didn't know you were interested in acting," her mom said, looking bemused.

"I didn't either, until today," said Zibby. "Auditions are tomorrow, so I'd better get practicing. I have to sing 'Happy Birthday.'"

Zibby poured herself a glass of milk. "Actually, I can start right now. Want to listen?"

"Sure," said her mom.

"Thure," echoed Sam with his toddler lisp.

The two sat down in kitchen chairs and looked expectantly at Zibby.

"All right," Zibby said, then cleared her throat. "Here I go." She opened her mouth and began to sing. But as she did, something strange happened. She felt so nervous, she could barely get any sound out of her lungs, and the one thing Zibby had always possessed, besides soccer skills, was a healthy set of lungs!

"Why don't you try again?" her mom asked. "This time, use that Zibby volume we know and love."

Zibby took a deep breath, then bellowed, *"Happy birthday to you ..."*

"Ooo-kay," her mom interrupted, covering her ears. "That's a little too much volume. Can you aim for a happy medium?"

Zibby bit her lips, reached down deep to find her inner performer, and sang the whole song not too loud, not too soft, but just right.

"Perfect," said her mom, smiling. "You're good! Really good. I must say that I'm surprised because your father's side of the family can't carry a tune at all. They're all tone deaf – why, your father can't even stay on key for 'Jingle Bells.' But my mom, your Grandma Betty, has a nice voice. She used to sing me the most beautiful lullabies. And I think she was in some musicals when she was a kid. It looks like you've inherited some of her talent."

"You think so?" asked Zibby, smiling. *So performing*

*runs in* my *family too!*

"I certainly do," said her mom.

"Thanks," said Zibby, feeling pretty good. But then she remembered Amber and she frowned. "But I think I'll go practice some more upstairs, just to be on the safe side."

By the time her mom called her to dinner, she'd sung "Happy Birthday" sixty-three more times. She knew the exact number because she kept a tally in her notebook.

"I am *so* prepared," she said to herself as she hurried downstairs and sat down at the dining room table.

Her dad was working late, but her mom, Sam, and her older brother, Anthony, were already seated at the table.

Just as Zibby reached for a sip of her water, Anthony called out, "Heads up!" and threw something in her lap.

"Anthony," her mom said in her Settle Down Voice.

"What is this?" Zibby asked, holding a baggy of something that resembled soap flakes.

"My fingernail clippings," said Anthony.

"Gross!" yelled Zibby, holding the baggy away from her as if it were a dead mouse. "Why would I want these?"

"Mom filled me in on your big audition and if you want to get the lead, *that* is your secret weapon," Anthony said, pointing to the baggy. "This guy on the track team carries his clippings with him. Ever since he started doing it, he's won every race. I collected mine last week and put them in my pocket so I would have them during a big freshman English exam, and I totally aced it. It really works – so I'm giving mine to you as a good luck charm."

"Thanks, I guess," she said hesitantly, still holding the baggy at arm's length.

"Zibby, will you *please* remove that disgusting item from the dining room table?" her mom asked.

"With pleasure!" Zibby said as she hurried into the kitchen. She was about to throw the baggy in the trash, despite its personal meaning for Anthony, when the phone rang.

"House of Zibby," she said as she picked it up.

"I just talked to Amber and you won't believe it," Sarah announced without bothering to say hi. "Her *voice teacher's* been over all night working with her on 'Happy Birthday.'"

"What?" said Zibby, her heart sinking. "She has a *voice teacher*?"

"I know, it's total overkill," said Sarah. "But I had to let you know in case you wanted to practice some more."

"But I've already practiced sixty-three times!" yelled Zibby. "I'm done practicing!"

"*Ziiiiibbbby*, please get off the phone. We're waiting for you!" her mom called from the dining room.

"Oh, shoot, gotta go. Thanks for the warning," said Zibby, hanging up the phone.

She started to throw away the baggy again, but then reconsidered.

*I'd better keep this*, she thought to herself, jamming the baggy into her pocket. Because if what Sarah said was true, she'd need all the luck in the world to beat Little Miss Voice Lessons tomorrow!

# CHAPTER 4

## AN AUDITION TO REMEMBER

"What *are* you wearing?" Zibby asked Amber the next day out on the blacktop before school. Amber, usually attired in a short skirt and fitted tee from Ambercrombie was dressed in a pink Nike shirt, pink and black athletic shorts, soccer cleats, and a pink headband adorned with little soccer balls.

"Did you see this?" Amber asked, ignoring Zibby's question and snapping her hair elastic. "Eeensy-weensy soccer balls!"

Zibby inspected Amber's hair more closely. It was true – even Amber's elastic was soccer-themed!

"Let me guess – you dressed up for the audition," said Zibby.

"Look the part, get the part," said Amber with a smile as she folded her arms across her chest.

Zibby glanced down at her own outfit – a striped tee and capri pants, paired with one of her black-and-white checkered Vans and one of Sarah's purple platform shoes. *Leave it to Amber to look 1,000 times more like a soccer player than the real one*, she thought, shaking her head.

"By the way, how about another soccer lesson

today?" asked Amber. She pointed to her feet. "My toes should be safe with these clunkers on."

"Sorry," Zibby said. "I wish I could help you, but I can't. I'm trying out for the role of Miranda myself."

Amber blinked. "But you said you weren't trying out!"

"I changed my mind," Zibby shrugged. "And I'm all set for the audition too."

"Wow," Amber said, shaking her head as if she hadn't heard right. Then she smiled. "Cool. You try out today and then after *I* get the role, you can coach me in soccer."

"Gee, and after *I* get the role, you can give me hair and makeup pointers," Zibby shot back.

"We'll just see about that," said Amber, stamping her foot and briskly walking away.

Zibby was glad when morning recess came because it meant she wouldn't have to stare at the Soccer Vision In Pink for a little while. Plus, she figured running around the soccer field would be a good distraction from thinking about the audition, which, she had to admit, was causing her stomach to turn like a Ferris wheel.

But today, soccer wasn't much fun. A new kid named Shiloh was playing on their team, and he kept hogging the ball. If he would have passed the ball two times, her team would have scored. But instead, he kept it for himself and made bad shots that missed the goal.

"You've got to pass!" Zibby said to him angrily after

he blew the second goal. "Matthew was totally open. So was I!"

Shiloh grunted at her. "I don't like passing."

"Soccer is a team sport. You can't do it all alone!" said Zibby.

"The way I play it you can," he grunted, and started to walk away.

"Then why don't you just take up golf instead!" yelled Zibby.

She clomped over to Matthew, who was standing in the center of the field getting ready for another kick off.

"Does that Shiloh have to play?" she asked. "He's such a jerk."

"I know," said Matthew. "But school rules – everyone plays."

He looked at her and then patted her on the shoulder. "Don't stress over it too much, tomboy," he said. "Save your energy for the audition this afternoon."

*The audition? Oh yeah*, remembered Zibby, feeling her stomach tense up again. At least Shiloh was good for one thing – he had successfully gotten her mind off the "Happy Birthday" competition for a little while!

* * *

The auditions that afternoon were held in the school auditorium, and the place was packed with sixth graders.

Zibby and Sarah grabbed seats, and Amber and Camille sat down right in front of them.

When Matthew walked into the auditorium, Amber whipped around.

"I'm so glad Matthew's trying out," she whispered to Zibby and Sarah. "He's such a cutie!"

"Totally!" agreed Camille, and the two girls began to giggle.

"And there they go again," Zibby muttered to herself.

After a few minutes, Mrs. Halpin, a large woman with flowing dark hair and an ankle-length polka-dotted skirt, stepped out onto the stage.

"I'd like to thank you all for coming to the auditions for *A Season of Change*," she smiled. "I'll be calling you up onto the stage one by one to sing 'Happy Birthday.' I'm also handing out a sheet that lists all the characters in the play and includes a brief description of each role. Before you sing, please tell me if there is one role you're interested in. I will keep your preference in mind when selecting the cast, but there's no guarantee you'll get it."

Zibby didn't even look at the handout. There was only one role she wanted and one alone! Sarah, however, studied the list of characters carefully.

"This sounds like a good part," she said to Zibby. "Deirdre, Miranda's loyal sidekick. That way, if you're Miranda, then we can be best friends in the play too."

"That would be awesome," said Zibby. She clasped

her hands together and looked up at the ceiling. "Please, drama gods, be kind to us!"

Mrs. Halpin took a seat in the front row, clipboard in hand, and began calling kids up to sing on stage, starting with the boys.

Zibby was so worried about her own upcoming performance that she couldn't focus very much on the boys, but she did notice one Very Big Obvious Thing: Matthew was by far the best. His voice was strong and clear, and he looked so comfortable on stage that it was as if he'd been performing his whole life.

"He's good," Zibby whispered to Sarah.

"I bet he gets the boy lead," said Sarah.

Next, Mrs. Halpin called up the girls. Sarah was one of the first to sing, and Zibby thought her voice sounded really pretty. So did Camille's. But a lot of the girls sang off-key, and some you could barely hear.

Finally, only Zibby and Amber were left to try out. Zibby pulled out the baggy of fingernails from her pocket and squeezed it for good luck just as Mrs. Halpin called her name. She leapt out of her seat and bounded up onto the stage so quickly, she didn't have time to stuff the baggy completely back into her pocket. It ended up falling on the floor, and the nails went everywhere.

"Just great," she said to herself quietly. "So much for these things being lucky!" She bent down and began to pick up the nails as quickly as possible. Two girls sitting in the front row jumped up to help her.

"What *are* these?" one of the girls asked, bending over and closely examining one of the clippings.

"They look like ... *fingernails!*" cried out the other girl, who dropped the fingernail she'd been holding and ran back to her seat. The other girl followed her, screaming, "Gross!" and the two shook their hands as if they were trying to get rid of some invisible bugs.

The other kids in the audience looked at each other with looks of horror on their faces, and Zibby could hear a muttering of "Yuck" and "Totally disgusting" float across the auditorium.

Zibby picked up the last clipping, dropped it in the baggy, and stuffed the whole thing back into her pocket. She straightened up and looked at Mrs. Halpin, who was giving her a Less-Than-Happy Stare.

"Distractions finally over?" Mrs. Halpin asked.

"Sorry," said Zibby, biting her lip.

"Then let the audition begin," Mrs. Halpin said.

Zibby took a deep breath. "I'm trying out for the part of Miranda," she said, then began to sing "Happy birthday to you." Her first line was a little wobbly due to the Fingernail Fiasco, but by the second line, she felt confident and in control. And by the end, she felt she'd sung the song her absolute best.

"I nailed it!" she said to herself under her breath. She then remembered what was in her pocket and gave the nail clippings a little squeeze, pleased by her own little pun. She smiled over at Mrs. Halpin, who nodded her head and then marked something down on her clipboard.

"Good job," she said to Zibby – something she hadn't said to any other girl yet that day!

"Thank you," Zibby said with a big grin, and then went back to her seat.

Now only Amber was left. After Mrs. Halpin called her name, Amber took her place on stage and flashed a mega-watt smile.

"First of all, thank you so much for coming here today," Amber said.

*As if everyone is here to watch you*, thought Zibby, shifting in her seat.

"I'm auditioning for the part of Miranda too," Amber continued. "But before I start, I need a little help from my friends."

From the back of the auditorium, two women walked down the center aisle and joined Amber on stage, one on each side. "I'd like to introduce to you Miss Wilkins, my wonderful voice teacher, and her dear friend Janey Pearson, a professional singer. They'll be backing me up today on vocals.

"On the count of one, two, three," said Amber, and then the trio launched into a version of "Happy Birthday" in perfect harmony, with Amber singing the melody and the two women filling in with "Ah-oohs."

By the time they hit the last note, Zibby was fuming. "That's cheating," she muttered to Sarah as Amber took a deep bow and the two women quickly stepped off stage. "No one else got to bring along backup singers."

"It's not fair," agreed Sarah.

Zibby glanced around to see if anyone else was miffed, but all the other kids erupted into wild applause. Some even gave Amber a standing ovation. And Mrs. Halpin was clapping so hard it looked as if her hands were going to fly off her wrists.

"This just isn't right," Zibby said to herself. "I'll show Amber. I'll show her she's not the only one who can break the rules to get the part."

*But how? How can I top Amber?*

And then, she got another one of her Very Good Ideas. She rushed out of the auditorium and onto the playground where she grabbed a soccer ball from the sporting equipment container. She raced back to the auditorium and onto the stage just as Amber was stepping down. Amber gave her a curious glance as they passed each other, but Zibby ignored her.

"Mrs. Halpin," Zibby called out. "I forgot part of my audition, and I want to show you right now."

Mrs. Halpin, still standing after her Crazy Clap Fest over Amber's audition, clutched her clipboard to her chest and frowned. "You've had your audition, Zibby. It was very good. But now it's time for us all to go home."

"Please," Zibby pleaded. "It'll only take a minute. I know Miranda is a soccer player, so you've got to see this." Without waiting for a reply from Mrs. Halpin, she began to dribble the ball deftly from her right to her left foot as she sang: "Happy birthday to you, happy birthday to you, happy birthday, happy birthday, happy birthday to you."

On the final "you," just to really impress everyone with her superior soccer skills, she booted the ball off the stage. She was aiming high and for the back row of the auditorium, but she didn't get enough height on the ball and instead, it headed right toward Mrs. Halpin. Mrs. Halpin quickly thrust her clipboard in front of her face to protect herself, and the force of the ball pushed her back into her seat as if she were a rag doll.

"*Oouf!*" she screamed as her clipboard clattered to the ground.

"Oh no," said Zibby, putting her hand to her mouth in horror as several kids ran over to see if Mrs. Halpin was all right. "What have I done?"

# CHAPTER 5

## NOT-SO-PRETTY IN PINK

The next afternoon in the auditorium while waiting for Mrs. Halpin to announce the cast members, Zibby slumped as far down in her seat as possible.

"Maybe if she can't see me, she'll forget I practically knocked her out yesterday," Zibby said to Sarah, who was sitting next to her. "There's no way she's going to give me the role of Miranda now."

"Don't worry so much," said Sarah. "She was totally fine – just a little shaken up, that's all. Besides, it was an accident. You were really good in your audition, and that's what counts."

"I guess so," said Zibby doubtfully.

Mrs. Halpin rushed into the auditorium and took her place in the center of the stage. The two girls stopped talking. Zibby slunk down even lower in her seat.

"Hello, fellow thespians," Mrs. Halpin said with a smile. "Today, I'll be announcing the cast for the play. First of all, let me thank each and every one of you for trying out. You were all terrific," she said as she beamed at them. "Of course, not everyone can get a lead role, or the specific role they want, but please know that every single part is important and vital to the play's success."

"Yeah, right," whispered Zibby to Sarah. "She's just saying that to let the losers down gently."

Mrs. Halpin continued. "I'll start by announcing the leads and then the members of the chorus." She looked down at a piece of paper attached to her clipboard.

"The role of Miranda will be played by," she paused dramatically, "Amber Stanton."

"No surprise there," Zibby whispered to Sarah. "She cheated *and* she didn't try to take off Mrs. Halpin's head."

"Thank you!" Amber squealed, jumping out of her seat and throwing a kiss to Mrs. Halpin. "Thank you so much!"

"And the role of the lead male, James," Mrs. Halpin continued, "will be played by Matthew Sheehan."

Matthew, sitting toward the front, turned red and gave a sheepish smile.

*That's great*, thought Zibby, clapping her hands together until they hurt. *He really deserves it.*

Zibby's hands got an even bigger workout a few seconds later when Mrs. Halpin announced that Sarah would be playing Deirdre.

"That's so great!" said Zibby, grinning at Sarah.

"Thanks," Sarah said, beaming back. But then she stopped smiling. "I just wish I could be *your* loyal sidekick rather than Amber's."

Zibby shrugged as if to say, "Don't worry about it."

But inside, *she* was worried. Not only didn't she get the role of Miranda, but it looked as if she might not get any speaking part at all! Camille got the role of the principal, Zane – a boy Zibby played soccer with – was Miranda's teacher, and even some girl who'd *forgotten* the words to "Happy Birthday" got a part as the school secretary!

*The play may be one team I'm not chosen for*, Zibby thought, feeling near tears.

But then, she heard her name.

"And Zibby Payne will play the role of 'Prissy Girl,'" announced Mrs. Halpin.

"Yes!" Zibby said to herself. "I made it! I got a part!"

But then, she backed up a minute. *What role did Mrs. Halpin say she was playing?*

"Could you repeat that, please?" Zibby asked, standing up.

"I said that you will be playing the role of 'Prissy Girl' in the script."

"That's the character's name?"

"No, that's the character she's portraying," explained Mrs. Halpin. "The character has no real name. She's just called 'Prissy Girl.'"

"You mean she's a *girly girl*?" Zibby asked, wrinkling her nose in disgust. "One who puts on makeup and plays with her hair and talks about how cute boys are all the time?"

"Exactly," Mrs. Halpin smiled. "I see that you already have a grasp of the character. Excellent!"

Zibby collapsed back into her seat.

"Can you believe it?" she asked Sarah. "Me? Playing *her*?"

"I'm sorry," Sarah said, looking as if she might cry on Zibby's behalf.

*But wait*, Zibby thought, sitting up straighter. Maybe the role wasn't set in stone yet.

She raised her hand. "Mrs. Halpin, are you sure I'm right for the role?"

"Of course I am," said Mrs. Halpin, looking up from her clipboard. "It's a great part. You get to sing your own solo."

"I do?" asked Zibby, perking up. "What's it called?"

"'Pink, Wonderful Pink,'" answered Mrs. Halpin. "It's a snappy little tune about how much fun it is to dress up in bows, ribbons, lace, and pastels. Prissy Girl is a very pivotal role. She's a crucial counterpart to sporty Miranda, and her song is one of the highlights of the show. I look forward to hearing you sing it," she said, and she turned her attention back to her cast list.

*Just great!* Zibby thought, slumping back into her seat. *I'm glad someone's looking forward to it. Because I'm definitely not!*

Mrs. Halpin finished reading the cast list as well as the members of the chorus and then informed everyone that the first practice would be tomorrow at three o'clock sharp.

"We have six weeks to get ready for this

production, and I know if we all work hard, we can do it," she said. "I'll be handing out scripts tomorrow, so see you all then," she finished, and with a wave, she exited the stage.

The students started jumping out of their seats and clumping together in small groups to talk excitedly about their parts in the play. Everyone except Zibby, that is. She just sat in her chair, chin down. Sarah tried to pull her up, but she refused.

"I just need some time to take this all in," Zibby said sullenly.

All of a sudden, Mrs. Halpin appeared back on stage and clapped her hands together wildly.

"Students, students!" she said. "I forgot to mention something. Something very important! I didn't tell you who the understudies are. I only assign them for the two main roles just to make sure we're covered if one of the leads gets sick or can't make a performance. So, I would like to announce that the understudy for Matthew is Zane Watkins. And Amber's understudy is Zibby Payne."

Zibby sat straight up in her seat and looked around. *Me? Amber's understudy? What does that mean exactly?* She ran up on stage to Mrs. Halpin.

"Excuse me, but if I'm Amber's understudy, does that mean I have to memorize all her lines?" she asked.

"Yes, dear, it's a very important job," replied Mrs. Halpin. "You need to be 100 percent ready, waiting in the wings so to speak, should Amber be unable to perform in the play."

"So you mean it's a lot of extra work, for nothing?" asked Zibby.

"It's not for nothing," Mrs. Halpin said, looking indignant. "You never know when and if you will be called to stand in and play Miranda. Plus, it is superb training for any young actress because you get so much more practice and experience than you normally would."

"Oh," Zibby said, sounding glum.

"Cheer up, dear," said Mrs. Halpin. "You'll always have 'Pink, Wonderful Pink' to sing," she said, and she turned her attention to another kid who was waiting to talk to her.

*Yeah, how cheery*, thought Zibby.

Zibby walked back down the stage, still a bit in shock, when she almost collided into Amber who was chatting with some girls at the bottom of the stage stairs.

"Congratulations," Zibby said, trying to be a good sport.

"Thanks," smiled Amber. "I just feel so sad you didn't get to be Miranda," she said, but her voice didn't sound sad, not one little bit, Zibby noticed. "But, since you *are* now my understudy," said Amber, "could you get me a bottle of water out of the Coke machine in the teacher's lounge? I'm super thirsty."

Zibby couldn't believe what she was hearing. "I'm your understudy, not your slave," she said crossly.

"Well, then, what about finding me a cup and getting some water for me out of the tap?" Amber persisted.

"No way," Zibby shook her head.

Amber sighed and kept on talking as if she hadn't heard Zibby. "Now listen, I gotta run because my dad is taking me to the BB5 concert tonight." BB5 was a new boy band Amber and Camille were obsessed with. "But I was talking to Mrs. Halpin, and she totally agreed that you should keep helping me with soccer. And since I can't do it right now, how about we get together tomorrow? Okay?"

Before Zibby could answer, Amber was halfway out the door. "Luv ya for it! Bye!" she chirped, and with a wave of her Red Hot Pink fingernails, she was gone.

*Ugh!* Now, not only did Zibby have to play a "prissy girl" and watch her best friend pretend to be Amber's best friend, she had to memorize a bunch of lines for a role she'd never get to play *and* be forced to teach Amber soccer. She hit her forehead with the palm of her hand. *Why* did she even try out for this play in the first place?

# CHAPTER 6

## A LUCKY BREAK

That night at home, Zibby's mom did her best to make Zibby feel better. "Maybe you'll find out you have more in common with 'Prissy Girl' than you think," she said, sitting on the edge of Zibby's bed where Zibby was curled up under a blanket.

"Yeah, right," she said sulkily.

"The thing about acting," her mom continued, "is that you don't play *yourself* – you play a *character*."

"But the whole reason I tried out was to play myself, or I mean, Miranda, who is just like myself!" she said.

"Have you even read the script yet?" her mom asked. "Maybe you'll learn that Miranda wasn't right for you anyway."

"Mom, no offense, but what do you know about it?" Zibby turned her face to the wall.

Her mom sighed and stood up. "I'll come back and check on you later."

"Fine," Zibby said in a muffled voice.

A few minutes passed, and then her dad knocked on her door.

"Hi, Zibs," he said softly, walking up to her bed.

"Hi, Daddy," she said, turning around from the wall to face him.

"I'm so proud of you for trying out for the play," he said. "That was a real stretch for you. And getting a speaking part – that's impressive."

Zibby shrugged. "But I didn't get the role I wanted."

"But at least you tried," he said encouragingly. "When I was your age, I never tried out for plays, probably because I wasn't any good at singing. During sixth-grade graduation, when our class was singing 'What a Wonderful World,' the teacher told me to just move my lips and pretend to sing, so that no one could hear me. I was that bad!"

"Poor you," Zibby said sympathetically.

"But you, Zibby, you can sing," he continued. "And Mom tells me you're singing a solo. That's something to look forward to. And when you're singing it, I'll be the proudest father in the entire audience."

Zibby gave him a little smile. "Thanks, Dad," she said. She really did feel a little better. Something about being around her father always cheered her up.

"What do you say we go out and get some ice cream to celebrate you being in the play?" he asked.

"All right," she said, throwing off the blanket and feeling a little bit happier. A scoop or two of Fudge Ripple would definitely take the edge off the day.

\* \* \*

The next day out at the blacktop before school started, Zibby nervously looked around for Amber. She really didn't feel like having Amber rub the whole understudy thing in her face again, and she especially didn't feel like giving her a soccer lesson. But she didn't see Amber anywhere. She wasn't even in class.

"Where's Amber?" Zibby whispered to Camille as Miss Cannon began passing out the day's assignments.

"I don't know," Camille replied. "Maybe sleeping in after the BB5 concert? I heard it went late – past midnight!"

"Nice parents," Zibby said, raising her eyebrows. "They let Amber go to a concert on a school night and then miss school?"

"I know," agreed Camille.

Personally, Zibby thought Amber was spoiled, but in this case it worked in Zibby's favor because she didn't have to worry about Amber bugging her.

At recess, Zibby ran out to the field to play soccer, hoping it would get her mind off the play. But when she joined the boys, she found them arguing.

"You want *this* ball?" Shiloh was saying, holding out a shiny new red one.

"Then I get to be team captain today."

Matthew looked uncomfortable. "I guess that's okay," he said.

"Great," said Shiloh, smirking. "Oh, and dudes, anyone on my team has to pass it to me every time I get near the goal, so I can take all the shots."

"That's not cool," said Matthew.

"That's the way it is, though," Shiloh said as he shrugged.

Matthew and the other boys looked at each other, then looked at the red ball. From the expressions on their faces, Zibby could tell they really wanted to play with a ball that wasn't half-flat and lopsided.

"Fine," Matthew sighed.

"Hey, that's not right!" said Zibby. She couldn't believe Matthew and the other boys were letting Shiloh bully them around like that.

"Forget it!" she said to Shiloh.

"Then you can forget about using my hand-stitched, authentic pro leather ball with a built-in pump," Shiloh said smugly, holding the ball over his head and out of her reach.

"Fine!" said Zibby, feeling herself heat up. "You can keep your stupid ball and play all by yourself!" Before she knew what she was doing, she leapt up and smacked the ball out his hands with her right palm. The ball went shooting down the field toward the classrooms.

Shiloh looked surprised, then quickly feigned a lazy smile. "Fine with me," he said. "Have fun playing with your cruddy old ball." He started to whistle and strolled off the field.

All the boys stared at Zibby.

"Sorry," she said, worried she'd ruined the game

for them.

Matthew walked over to her. "Don't worry about it," he said. "It's not your fault."

He picked up the school ball and spun it on his right index finger. "This ball isn't so bad anyway. So let's get playing, tomboy," he said, smiling. "Or should I start calling you 'Prissy Girl,'" he teased.

"You'd better not!" Zibby exclaimed, slugging him on the shoulder. "Unless you want me to aim the ball for your head!"

"Don't pull a Mrs. Halpin on me, please," he said, referring to Zibby's now famous Audition Kick. "I take it back!" he said, running out on the field.

"I thought so!" she said, following behind him, laughing.

* * *

At play practice that afternoon, Amber was still nowhere to be seen.

"Where could she be?" Zibby asked Sarah. "I can't believe she'd miss the first day of practice."

"Me either," said Sarah, looking around the room for her.

Mrs. Halpin walked onto the auditorium stage and clapped her hands together to get everyone's attention.

"Welcome, all of you, to the first day of rehearsal. I have an announcement to make. Last night, Amber broke her right foot and she'll be in a cast and on crutches for quite some time. So she will be unable to take on the lead role. And this means that Zibby Payne will become Miranda. And you, Jessica," she said, pointing to a girl sitting in the second row with brown hair, "will come out of the chorus to take on the role of Prissy Girl. Congratulations, Zibby and Jessica."

Zibby's mouth fell open. What? Did she hear that right? She was Miranda? She got the part after all?

"This is the Most Awesome Day of My Life," she started to scream, but surprisingly, nothing came out of her mouth. The world started to move in slow motion and her vision grew fuzzy and narrow. And she had the very strangest sensation in her head – it was as if crickets were chirping in her brain. And maybe Zibby had more in common with Prissy Girl than she thought, because she – supposed tough tomboy – fell back into her chair and fainted!

# CHAPTER 7

## A SURPRISE ENDING

"Zibby, are you all right?" Sarah asked, bending over her and fanning Zibby's forehead with her script. Mrs. Halpin was standing right behind her.

"Everyone clear away," Mrs. Halpin said. She gently pushed back some girls who were crowding in to get a look at Zibby.

"What?" Zibby asked groggily. "What's happening?"

"Mrs. Halpin announced that you're now Miranda. And you fainted," Sarah said.

"I'm Miranda?" Zibby asked. She shook her head and began to see – and think – clearly again. "I'm Miranda!" And she stood up and began jumping around.

"*Whoa*, not so fast," said Mrs. Halpin, holding Zibby by the shoulders. "Sit down – you shouldn't move around so much after you faint." Then she helped Zibby into her seat.

"I'm fine," protested Zibby.

"Hmm," said Mrs. Halpin, her eyes narrowing. "Do you faint a lot?"

"No," said Zibby. "This was the first time."

"Do you often feel sick, dizzy, breathless, or

woozy?" Mrs. Halpin persisted.

"No!" exclaimed Zibby.

Mrs. Halpin stared at her. "I'm just worried you don't have the constitution – the strength – to take on such a taxing role as Miranda."

Zibby popped out of her seat. "Strength? What are you talking about? I'm, like, the strongest girl in sixth grade." And before Mrs. Halpin could stop her, Zibby hit the floor and began doing push-ups in the aisle.

After she'd completed ten, she leapt back up. "Want to go outside and watch me run a few laps?" she asked. "I can run an eight-and-a-half-minute mile, even when I'm wearing two different kinds of shoes."

Mrs. Halpin held up her hand in protest. "All right, dear, you've proven your point. After all, I shouldn't be questioning your physical prowess – not after that kick of yours at the audition. I'll presume your fainting was a one-time fluke, but you should see the school nurse first thing in the morning."

Mrs. Halpin turned to address the rest of the kids. "Now if everyone will give me a second, I need to go get the scripts out of my office. No more fainting while I'm gone," she said as she stepped out the door.

As soon as she left, Sarah and Zibby turned to each other and gave the biggest simultaneous scream of their lives. "Now we can be best friends in real life *and* in the play," said Zibby, breathless after all the screaming. "Just like we wanted!"

"But I do wonder what exactly happened to Amber," Zibby said, looking around. "Does anyone know?"

"No," replied Camille, who was sitting next to them. "But I'm about to find out," she said as she whipped out her cell phone.

"Hello?" Camille shouted into the phone. "Amber? How *are* you? Oh ... oh ... terrible! Awful! The worst! You poor thing," Camille said, nodding sympathetically.

"Yes," she continued. "Mrs. Halpin told her." Camille looked at Zibby, and then continued. "She's thrilled. Totally."

Zibby looked at Camille expectantly.

Camille covered the phone receiver with her hand. "She wanted to know how you're feeling about being Miranda," she whispered to Zibby.

"Oh," said Zibby, giving a big smile and a thumbs up.

Camille turned her attention back to the phone. "Yes. Of course. I'll tell her. Get better, babe. Luv ya. Kisses." Camille puckered up her lips and smooched into the phone twice, then snapped the phone shut.

She turned to face Zibby. "Amber says to not freak out because you're taking over from her – just do your best, even if you can't ever be as good as she would have been."

"How thoughtful of her," said Zibby, rolling her eyes.

"So what happened?" asked Sarah, eager to get the scoop.

"You know how she went to the BB5 concert last night?" continued Camille. "After the concert, her dad said she could go to the back door to get autographs. While she was waiting, she took out her lip gloss and was putting it on when the door opened and BB5 appeared. She got so excited, she dropped the lip gloss. Then, the crowd started chasing the band, and as Amber started to run along with them, she tripped on her lip gloss that was rolling on the ground and fell. And that's how she broke her foot."

*Wow,* thought Zibby. *A makeup casualty. That has to be a first!*

"She's devastated," said Camille. "When she told the doctor about being in the play, he said, 'No way.' She's not even supposed to move for a few days while waiting for the bone to set, and she's going to be in a cast for up to a month!"

"Poor thing," said Sarah, looking sympathetic.

*More like 'silly thing,'* thought Zibby. She did feel bad for Amber for missing out on getting to play Miranda, but on the other hand, she couldn't help but think that that's what she gets for caring so much about makeup!

Mrs. Halpin returned with a stack of scripts and handed them out, starting with Zibby and Matthew.

"This is the most beautiful thing I've ever seen," Zibby said to herself as she reverently touched the cover, which was red with gold lettering. Someone had written her name in big block letters on it. "Zibby" was actually written *over* the name "Amber," but Zibby didn't mind. The new Miranda held her script up tightly to her chest as if someone were going to rip it away from her.

Mrs. Halpin handed out the rest of the scripts, as well as a rehearsal schedule, then gave a lecture on her expectations of them as well as the rules they'd have to follow while using the auditorium. She then checked her watch.

"It's already four thirty," she said. "That's a wrap for today. Look over your scripts tonight, please, and we'll start again tomorrow at three o'clock."

Before Zibby headed home, she borrowed Sarah's cell phone to call her mom and tell her the good news. When she got home, she found her mom *and* dad waiting at the door.

"What are you doing here?" she asked her dad. "You're home so early."

"I rushed home from work to take the star of the show out to dinner," he said. "I thought we'd celebrate at the Steak Shack."

"Yum," said Zibby. "Can I get French onion soup?"

"Whatever the actress wants, the actress gets," said her dad.

"Wow, thanks!"

"We'll leave in about a half hour," her mom said. "We're just waiting for Anthony to get home."

"Cool," said Zibby. "That gives me some time to look over my lines."

She ran up to her room, flopped on the bed, and pulled out her script. She couldn't wait to see what Miranda was going to do!

She flipped through the pages, approvingly skimming the story line about how Miranda starts a new school, uses soccer to fit in and win friends, and then helps her team win the school's first soccer championship in thirty years.

"This plot rocks," Zibby said to herself. "Mrs. Halpin is a genius!"

She skipped to the final scene where the principal announces Miranda and the rest of the team to the school at a huge pep rally. Then James, the most popular boy in school, presents Miranda with the Most Valuable Player trophy, and then he leans down and ...

*"What?"* shouted Zibby.

She read the script again. "Where did *that* come from?" she asked herself. "This can't be right. Mrs. Halpin is crazy!"

Zibby thought back to what her mom had said the day before, about how maybe the role of Miranda might not be a good fit for her. Well, had her mom ever been right about that!

Because there on page 83 was the Most Horrible, Terrible Scene Ever Written:

"James leans down and kisses Miranda."

Zibby slammed the script shut and buried it in her backpack, wishing she could hide it for good somewhere.

"Cancel the dinner!" she called downstairs to her parents. "I've lost my appetite!"

# CHAPTER 8

## A KISS TO BE MISSED

The next day at school, Zibby ran up to Sarah on the blacktop and thrust the script in front of her face. "Check it out," said Zibby. "Page 83."

"Oh, yeah," Sarah grimaced. "I saw that late last night. I had a feeling you'd be freaking."

"It's so wrong for so many reasons I can barely count them," exclaimed Zibby. "I'm a tomboy, and tomboys don't kiss boys! Plus, kissing is totally gross. Third, I've known Matthew forever and I even remember when he ate a worm on the playground in first grade. And you think I'm going to kiss him now?"

"Well, I'm sure he hasn't eaten any worms lately," said Sarah sensibly.

"And what would happen on the soccer field," Zibby continued, ignoring Sarah's comment. "How can we play soccer together when we have to *kiss* each other? It will wreck everything! How could I ever face him on the field again?"

"It's a problem," agreed Sarah.

"A humongous one!" exclaimed Zibby. "I've got to talk to Matthew about it right now!" She closed the script and put it under her arm.

Zibby ran across the schoolyard to where Matthew was talking to Zane and some other friends.

"Have you looked at the script yet?" she asked Matthew.

"A little," he replied. "Not the whole thing."

"Well," she said, grabbing his arm and leading him away from the other boys. "Take a look at this on page 83," she demanded. She opened up the script. "Right there!" she pointed halfway down the page.

Matthew read the passage, then gulped. And promptly turned red. "Oh," he said.

"I know that as actors we're supposed to be *professionals*, but I'm telling you I'm not gonna do this!"

"It's not like I want to do it either," said Matthew huffily.

"Of course not," Zibby snapped. "So we've got to do something to get out of it," she said, staring off into space, thinking. "I know! We'll talk to Mrs. Halpin and get her to change the script. She'll do it – she has to. After all, we're the stars."

"Good idea," said Matthew. "Let's go find her – she's probably in the teacher's lounge."

He set off toward the lounge, with Zibby following. Once there, Matthew hesitated for a second in front of the door, so Zibby swung it open so hard it slammed against the inside wall. Immediately, about twenty teachers turned to look at her.

"Um, sorry to interrupt," Zibby said, smiling bravely. "We're looking for Mrs. Halpin."

"Over here," Mrs. Halpin cried out, waving from across the room where she was bent over the copying machine. She smiled when she saw Zibby and Matthew.

"Hello, dears," she said cheerily. "How can I help you?"

Zibby rushed up to her. "We need to talk to you right away about the play, please."

"Sure," said Mrs. Halpin. "Anything for the lead characters!"

"*In private*," Zibby added, looking at her pleadingly.

Mrs. Halpin gave her a quizzical look and then said, "Okay. We can go outside if you like."

The minute the three were out the door and in the hallway, Zibby exploded,

"Matthew and I are very concerned about the script and that certain thing the two main characters have to do!"

"What thing?" asked Mrs. Halpin.

"*You know*," said Zibby.

"Yeah, *you know*," mumbled Matthew.

"No, I don't know," said Mrs. Halpin. "The main characters do a lot of things in the play."

"Here," Zibby opened up the script to page 83 and pointed. "*That* thing."

"Oh," Mrs. Halpin nodded her head knowingly. "The kiss."

Zibby grimaced at the mention of the word. Matthew turned red and looked away.

"Nothing to worry about, my dears," said Mrs. Halpin, closing the script. "It's a stage kiss. Not a real one. And you're not kissing each other. Miranda, the character, is kissing James, the character. You'll be fine."

"But Mrs. Halpin," said Zibby, "I just don't feel comfortable you-know-what-ing with Matthew. And he doesn't feel comfortable with it either, right Matthew?"

"Right," he said nodding his head vigorously.

Mrs. Halpin sighed. She motioned to a bench.

"Let's have a seat, shall we?" she asked.

They all sat down, with Zibby and Matthew to the left of Mrs. Halpin. "First of all, this kiss is very important to the play. It's a dramatic highlight, the culmination of Miranda and James's budding relationship throughout the play. The audience expects a kiss. In fact, the audience *demands* a kiss. The play won't work without one."

The two looked at her, unconvinced. So she continued, "Look, when I was your age, I was cast as Sandy in *Grease*. The boy I hated most in school, a mean kid named Paul Rawlings, was cast as Danny. We had been mortal enemies since kindergarten. During the drive-in movie scene, I had to kiss him."

She paused and looked at Zibby and Matthew. "Seconds before I was to kiss him on opening night, he muttered 'Fatso' under his breath to me. Oh, I wanted to slug him. But instead, I gave him a very convincing kiss. A kiss like I was crazy about him!

"And in part because of that kiss, I won best actress that year for our school district. Now *that's* called acting. And I know you two will be up for the challenge."

"But ..." Zibby started to say.

Mrs. Halpin stood up. "No more about this, please. I will see you two at rehearsal this afternoon." She started to walk back to the teacher's lounge when she stopped and turned around. "And oh, I didn't even tell you the worst thing about that kiss – Paul Rawling's breath smelled like rotten tuna fish!" she said, and then opened the door and disappeared.

Zibby and Matthew exchanged a look of horror.

"Umm, gotta go," mumbled Matthew, jumping off the bench and hurrying away.

"Rotten tuna fish?" Zibby said to herself. *Oh no!* She'd never stopped to think about what Matthew's breath might smell like if they kissed. Or what hers would smell like either. She loved tuna fish sandwiches. She also ate a lot of other stinky foods like dill and salmon and sometimes even sardines.

*This is awful,* she thought, burying her head in her hands. *Completely, utterly, hopelessly awful!*

# CHAPTER 9

## A SLIGHT REWRITE

That day at lunch, as Zibby was eating a cucumber and smoked salmon sandwich at the lunch tables with Sarah – and resisting the urge to cup her hand in front of her mouth, breathe, and do a smell check – Zibby heard a funny sucking sound. She looked around and saw Drew and Stephen, two boys she played soccer with, pursing their lips together and smooching the air.

"Oh, Matthew, I *loooooove* you," said Drew in a fake falsetto voice.

"Kiss, kiss."

"And Zibby, I love you," said Stephen, lowering his voice to make it deeper. "Kissy, kissy," he said, puckering up his lips grotesquely.

Zibby's eyes widened in horror. *Oh no. They must know about the script – about the kiss!* Normally she could care less what anyone thought of her, but this was different. Her tomboy reputation was on the line. And nobody messed with that.

"They must be stopped," she muttered to Sarah under her breath. She grabbed some straws lying on the table, marched over to where the boys were sitting, and began whipping them on their heads and shoulders with the straws.

"Cut it out, cut it out, cut it out!" she cried. "Right now!"

Drew and Stephen put their hands over their heads to protect themselves and started laughing. "Don't hurt me!" said Drew.

"And definitely don't kiss me!" said Stephen as they ran off.

"Losers!" Zibby yelled after them.

Sarah came up to her and patted her arm reassuringly.

"How did they know about the kiss when they're not even in the play?" Zibby asked.

"I don't know," shrugged Sarah. "I guess everyone read their scripts last night and word got around," she speculated.

Zibby started to pace back and forth. "I was going to go play soccer after I ate, but I don't want to run into Drew or Stephen again," she said.

"Stick with the girls today. We're nicer anyway," said Sarah.

She began to lead Zibby over to a crowd of girls at one of the lunch tables when Zibby noticed they were all laughing and pointing at her.

"What's going on?" Zibby asked.

"Nothing," said Camille, who was sitting right in the middle.

"Come on," said Zibby.

"Well, it's just that ... tell us, what does Matthew kiss like?" asked a girl named Laura. "Are his lips smooth? Rough?"

"Is he a wet kisser?" asked a girl named Jennifer who was wearing a Hello Kitty hair band.

"Does he look even cuter close up?" said Camille, giggling.

"What's it like to have him as your boyfriend?" piped up a girl named Vanessa, who was sitting at a nearby table. Vanessa had wrecked Zibby's tomboy club earlier in the year, and Zibby had never forgiven her.

"What are you talking about?" yelled Zibby. "We're only in the play together! That's it. He is not my boyfriend. We have not kissed. We are never going to kiss. So please stop asking me all these questions! Got it?" she said, looking straight at Vanessa.

"*Geesh.* Got it," said Vanessa, looking offended.

"Look who's being the temperamental drama queen," whispered Camille loudly enough so Zibby could hear. The girls all leaned in together and started whispering again.

"This kiss is killing me!" Zibby said to Sarah.

Sarah put her arm around her. "I'm so sorry," she said. "You'll be okay. Somehow."

*That's right, I will!* Zibby thought to herself, and then got one of her Very Good Ideas. *In fact, I'm gonna do something about that kiss right now.*

She said a quick goodbye to Sarah, then ran out to the soccer field to find Matthew. There he was, selecting his team.

"Emergency, emergency!" Zibby called out to him, waving her arms back and forth.

Matthew ran over to her with a questioning look on his face. But before he could ask what was happening, Zibby said, "We've got to get out of that scene! The whole idea of that you-know-what at the end of the play is so stupid, we should just rewrite the scene ourselves."

"But Mrs. Halpin says there has to be a ... you know ..." said Matthew.

"Hey, we're the leads and she should let us do what we want," said Zibby. "Besides, the script will be a lot better without that, um, thing in it. She'll see." Then she filled Matthew in on her Big Idea.

* * *

At rehearsal that afternoon, Mrs. Halpin asked the cast to run through the entire script. "Don't worry about saying your lines perfectly," she said. "But please follow the script carefully."

And everyone did, including Zibby and Matthew, even when they hit page 83.

Zibby faithfully read her line: "Thank you all for your support. Winning the championship has been the biggest highlight of my life, and winning it for the school makes the victory even sweeter."

Then Matthew read: "And I'd like to present you with the Most Valuable Player trophy."

Zibby read: "Thank you so much."

Matthew read: "And I'd also like to present you with this."

But when Zibby and Matthew got to the next line of stage direction – "James leans down and kisses Miranda" – they made their change. They leaned in close, looked deep into each other's eyes, and ... stuck out their hands and gave each other a hearty handshake.

"*Cut!*" roared Mrs. Halpin.

# CHAPTER 10

## A DRAMATIC TURN OF EVENTS

"Hey!" Mrs. Halpin yelped as she ran over. "That was supposed to be a kiss!"

"I'm not you-know-what-ing him," exclaimed Zibby. "I told you that already!"

Mrs. Halpin pressed her lips together and then looked at the rest of the cast. "Everyone but Zibby and Matthew, please go outside for a ten-minute break."

After the others left the auditorium, Mrs. Halpin put one arm around Matthew and the other around Zibby. "I know this is hard," she said. "So maybe what we should do is schedule a special practice session, just the three of us, where you can rehearse the kiss in private. Then when you do it on stage, it won't feel so strange." She squeezed their shoulders, then released them.

"You mean, do that thing more than I already have to?" asked Zibby, her eyes widening.

"Well, yes, dear," said Mrs. Halpin. "But each time it will get easier."

"No way!" said Zibby.

Matthew, now bright red, didn't say anything. He looked down at the floor and kicked an imaginary piece of dirt with his toe.

Mrs. Halpin sighed again. "Look, the kiss is in the final scene of the play, so let's skip it for the next few weeks and try again right before the dress rehearsal. Hopefully as you get into your characters more, you'll feel more comfortable with the kiss."

"Great idea!" said Zibby enthusiastically, even though she knew she'd never feel comfortable page 83-ing Matthew. But all that mattered to her was that at least for a few weeks, she didn't have to think about that stupid you-know-what!

The next day, Amber came back to school with a pink cast from her knee to her toes. The timing couldn't have been better for Zibby: Everyone was so wrapped up in Amber, they lost interest in teasing Zibby about The Kiss.

At lunch, the custodian rolled out an oversized reading chair from the library with a matching ottoman for Amber to sit on, because she couldn't fit her cast into the small space between the lunch bench and the table. From her perch, Amber barked out orders to the few kids she deemed worthy enough to sign her cast.

"Best handwriting only, no drawings unless I preapprove the sketches, and no black markers because black is just such a downer of a color and my mood is very fragile right now.

"Zibby, want to sign?" she asked, waving a packet of fruit-scented markers in front of her. "My *best* friends get to sign with these special pens."

"No thanks," said Zibby. "My handwriting's too messy," she fibbed. Zibby could have neat handwriting when she tried, but Amber's attitude made her not want to sign the cast at all.

When later that day Amber showed up to rehearsal, Zibby was worried that she was going to make a Big Scene and somehow try to get the part of Miranda back. But Mrs. Halpin gave Amber the new role she created of an injured soccer player, and Amber was treating it as if it were the Greatest Part Ever Written, even though she said only one word: "Ouch."

"The role is really so much more complex and layered than you might at first think," Amber said to Zibby. "Small roles really are the best – and so challenging for an actress."

"Right," smiled Zibby.

Amber was sad about one thing, however. "I really wish I got to kiss that cute Matthew though!" she said wistfully to Zibby.

About that, Zibby could finally agree with Amber. *I wish you could be the one to kiss him too!* She thought to herself.

The next four weeks flew by quickly. Zibby's days were filled with school and rehearsal; her nights were spent doing homework and memorizing her lines. And as each day whizzed by, the kiss grew fuzzier and fuzzier in Zibby's memory. It was almost as if there hadn't ever been one!

But of course, it did exist. Finally the day came, all too soon for Zibby, when Mrs. Halpin took Zibby and Matthew aside at a Thursday practice and told them that the next day, they'd be rehearsing the kiss.

"I hope you're ready for the final scene," she said. "The dress rehearsal's coming up in a little over a week, so we don't have any more time to waste."

Zibby gulped. Silently, she and Matthew walked out of the auditorium together. Then Matthew took Zibby's arm and exclaimed, "*Now* what are we going to do?"

"Stall?" she said tentatively.

"How?" he said. "We're doing the scene tomorrow."

"I don't know," said Zibby. "All I know is I'm not doing it." She started to walk away.

"But we have to," said Matthew as he grabbed her by the arm again. "Mrs. Halpin isn't going to change her mind. Besides, it's not that big of a deal. I talked to my uncle and he kisses women all the time on stage. Tomorrow, let's just do it and not think about it too much. It's just one kiss."

"One too many," Zibby said heatedly.

Matthew stopped walking. "You're so stubborn!" he yelled.

"I am not!" she yelled back.

Matthew shook his head and stomped off down the street.

*What's* his *problem*, Zibby thought as she walked home. *I don't care what his stupid uncle thinks – how could Matthew ever think that this would be okay?*

When Zibby got home, she moped around her room, unable to concentrate on her homework or anything else. Finally, she knocked on Anthony's door, which was half-open and gave it a little push. Anthony was lying on his bed, reading a Zits comic book.

"What's up?" he asked, looking at her.

"Have you ever kissed a girl?" she blurted out. She figured his answer would be yes. He'd had a girlfriend, Ashley, for a few months.

"That's kinda personal, isn't it?" he asked.

"Yeah, well ..." her voice trailed off.

"Why do want to know?"

"I'm supposed to kiss Matthew in the play," she said. "But I don't want to do it."

"Your first kiss ever – and on stage," Anthony said, nodding. "You're in big trouble!"

"I know," said Zibby.

"Well, yeah, I *have* kissed a girl," said Anthony. "And it's not too bad. Really. The first few times my lips bled, but after that, I got used to the taste of blood."

"No way!" Zibby exclaimed.

"Just kidding."

"Thanks a lot," she said huffily.

"You'll be fine," he said. "I promise. Don't worry about it. You just press your lips against his and ..."

Just as Zibby was about to plug her ears so she wouldn't have to hear any more details about the mechanics of kissing, she was saved by the ringing of the doorbell.

"Someone's here," she called out, turning and racing out of Anthony's room. She ran downstairs and opened the door. It was Matthew.

"Hi," she said, surprised to see him. "Are you going to yell at me some more?"

"No," he said. "It's just that ..." he stared down at the ground.

"Just what?" she asked.

"Just that ..." and then he grabbed hold of Zibby by the shoulders and tried to kiss her on her lips!

*"What are you doing?"* she screamed, batting him away.

"Kissing you so we could get it over with and so that you'll do it in the play," he said, turning red, yet again. "I figured if we kissed once, you'd see it wasn't so bad and you'd be okay with it."

"Well, you figured wrong!" Zibby yelled.

"Well, I'm sorry then!" he yelled back. "I guess I was stupid enough to even think you might like it!" His voice then grew softer. "I guess I was stupid enough to think I might like it!"

*What?* Zibby's mouth dropped. Was he saying he wanted to kiss her? She looked around, making sure no one had witnessed the Great Kissing Attempt, and then slammed the door.

*Oh no! Does this mean Matthew* likes *me? Likes me that way? This makes everything worse! A zillion times worse! There's no way I'm ever going to go through with this kiss!*

# CHAPTER 11

## A MAJOR PLOT CHANGE

That night in her room, Zibby wrote up a plan – a Do Or Die Anti-Kiss Scheme that would ensure that her two lips never touched Matthew's. And the next morning, she couldn't wait to get to school to launch it.

Before class, she dropped by the prop room in the basement of the auditorium. During one of the rehearsals, she'd once seen something that she could use. She rummaged through the boxes of clothes, costume jewelry, fake weapons, and wigs until she found the item she was looking for and she stuffed it in her pocket. She also grabbed a box of Kleenex that Mrs. Halpin kept on the counter.

As she exited the auditorium, she almost ran into Matthew, who was walking to class from the other direction. She looked down at the ground as they passed, and so did he.

*Talk about awkward*, she thought to herself. *Oh well*, she thought, trying to look at the bright side. She hoped that once she got that kiss out of her life, she and Matthew could get back to being friends and could forget all about that "liking each other" stuff!

* * *

During play rehearsal that afternoon, when the cast got to page 83, Zibby began to cough vigorously.

"I've come down with a terrible cold," Zibby said, speaking through her nose so that it sounded as if it were stuffed up. She pulled out a tissue and gave a big fake nose blow. "I'm a totally gross germ bag."

"That's strange. You weren't coughing in class today," Matthew said skeptically.

"I just got it," said Zibby. "It's one of those speed colds going around. You get it within minutes."

"Well, let's hope you lose this cold as quickly as you got it, because the final scene is up, dear," said Mrs. Halpin. "Right *now*."

Zibby took a deep breath as Matthew read his line before the kiss: "And I'd like to present you with this." Then, as he leaned toward her, she burst into another coughing fit.

"I can't go on any longer," she said dramatically. "I might get Matthew sick, and then he'd have to be hospitalized and he wouldn't be able to finish the play."

"Cut the coughing," Mrs. Halpin said firmly. "And if Matthew gets sick, his parents can send me the doctor's bill." She put her hands on her hips and waited.

*Shoot,* thought Zibby. Part One of her plan had failed. But no worries: She'd come prepared with a Plan B!

She fished around in her pocket and pulled out the

item she'd taken from the prop room – a set of fake wax lips. When Matthew read his line, she slapped the fake lips over her own and leaned in to kiss him.

Matthew backed away, startled. Mrs. Halpin yelled, "Take those lips off immediately!"

Zibby ripped the lips off and protested. "I'm sorry, but I told you – I'm concerned about Matthew's health. I don't want to get him sick. These lips will act as a germ barrier. I'm a very considerate person, that's all."

Mrs. Halpin stuck out her hand and said, "Lips, please."

Zibby handed the spit-covered prop over.

"We'll try the scene one more time," Mrs. Halpin said, wrapping the lips in a couple of tissues. "Correctly."

Mrs. Halpin turned to Matthew. "Please say your line again."

Matthew nodded, and said, "And I'd also like to present you with this."

Once again, he leaned toward Zibby and she ... leapt up!

"I can't do it. I just can't do it!" she cried out.

"You *can* do it," said Mrs. Halpin in a Very Irritated and Growing More-So Voice. "It's now or never."

"Then it's never," said Zibby. "Because I *quit*!" And with that, she ran off the stage.

# CHAPTER 12

## BAD REVIEWS

*Yes!* Zibby thought on the way home from school. *I'm free, finally free of that kiss!* Sure, she had to go to drastic lengths to get out of it, but the rewards would be well worth it.

At home later that evening, she helped her mom do the dishes without even being asked. She read three books to Sam and didn't get mad when Anthony teased her about The Kiss – because she knew there wasn't going to be one anymore!

Over the weekend, she didn't tell her family that she'd quit the play because she hated to disappoint them. She knew how much her parents were looking forward to seeing her perform. She'd tell them Monday. Or the next day. Right now, she just wanted to bask in the feeling of smooch-free relief!

\* \* \*

Monday morning at school, she ran up to Sarah on the blacktop.

"I'm *so* happy!" she exclaimed, expecting Sarah to

congratulate her. But instead Sarah stared at her icily and said, "Well, I'm not."

"Why?" asked Zibby, surprised. Sarah knew how much Zibby was dreading The Kiss – she should be thrilled for her!

"Did you ever stop to think that now somebody else has to play Miranda?" Sarah asked. "That someone has to memorize all her lines and songs, with the dress rehearsal this Saturday afternoon and the show opening up next Wednesday … *nine* days away."

"Oh," said Zibby. She hadn't really thought about that.

"Well, that someone is me," continued Sarah. "*I'm* Miranda now. Mrs. Halpin was going to give the role back to Amber because she just got her cast off, but she's still limping. Plus, the doctor says she still has to take it easy. And I hardly have any time to learn my lines! And, I'm a total klutz when it comes to soccer, which makes it even harder for me!"

"I'm sorry," Zibby said. And she was. She never meant to hurt Sarah.

"And don't forget that I now have to do the kiss for you!" Sarah said. "And Camille has to take over for me and learn a bunch of new lines, and that means that Franny Dewberry from chorus has to learn Camille's part, and she's terrible!" Sarah continued. "It's all a big fat mess, and it's all your fault! Mrs. Halpin says this may be the worst play she's ever put on!"

"But," Zibby sputtered, "that kiss was wrecking my life. I didn't have a choice!"

"Well, now it's wrecking everyone else's," said Sarah, and she stomped away.

Zibby sat down on the ground, despite the fact that the asphalt would leave gravel imprints on the backs of her legs. "Maybe I should have thought this through," she said to herself, looking around, wondering who else was mad at her.

She didn't have to wait long to find out. The next things she saw were two pairs of plum-colored ballet flats stemming from two sets of black leggings. She didn't even have to look up to see who it was. Amber and Camille. They often wore the same shoes.

"So the Oscar goes to ... Zibby Payne! Winner of the Most Selfish Actress award," said Amber dramatically.

Zibby still didn't look up.

"How could you do this to us?" asked Camille.

Zibby tried to explain, but before she could get a word out of her mouth, the two sets of ballet flats marched on.

* * *

In class later, Zibby wanted to talk to Matthew, but he was helping the principal with something until recess. Zibby was hoping that he, unlike the girls, would understand her position, and in fact be relieved because now that the Kissing Craziness was behind them, they could be friends again.

"Hey, Matthew," she said, and waved when she joined him out on the soccer field at recess. Getting out there together on the field and assisting each other with some goals would be a great way to celebrate Things Being Back To Normal.

But instead of greeting her with his usual "Hi, tomboy," he turned his back on her.

She tapped him on the back of the shoulder. "Matthew?"

He whirled around. "You can't play," he said.

"What?" she asked. "Everyone plays."

"Not you," he said flatly. "No quitters allowed on the field."

"Hey, if you're talking about the play, I didn't quit," she exclaimed. "I was forced out."

"You quit," said Matthew. "I heard it. So did everyone else."

"Well, I ..." Zibby stammered. Okay, so maybe technically she *had* quit. But was it her fault Mrs. Halpin wouldn't change the script?

"Okay, so I quit," she admitted. "Anyone would have in my position."

"You think so?" asked Matthew, turning so red he looked almost purple. "I don't. I don't think any other girl would have minded so much. Only you. You know what, Zibby? You can be a real pain. I guess that's where you got your name!"

Zibby felt the tears start to well up in her eyes. She turned around so Matthew couldn't see and wiped her eyes with the back of her hand. Slowly she headed back to the lunch tables, hoping she could duck into the bathroom before anyone could notice she'd been crying. But before she could reach the bathroom, Franny Dewberry, the girl who had taken over the role of principal, came running over to her.

"I love you!" she squealed, throwing her arms around Zibby. "Because of you, I have a speaking role. I'm so excited. I'm thrilled. My parents are thrilled. My grandparents are thrilled. So thank you, thank you, *thank you!*" She hugged Zibby one more time and then skipped away happily.

*At least someone's not mad at me,* Zibby thought, relieved. And for the first time since arriving at school, she didn't feel quite so bad about her decision.

* * *

When she got home from school, her mom met her at the front door.

"Guess what I did today?" she asked.

"Went to the store and got me a bunch of new friends that don't hate my guts?" answered Zibby.

"Huh?" asked her mom. "What are you talking about?"

"Nothing," shrugged Zibby.

"Today," her mom continued, "I went to the school and bought *fifteen* tickets to the play."

She pulled the tickets out of her pocket and fanned them out in front of Zibby. "We've invited everyone. Grandma Betty and Aunt Alexa and Uncle Robert, and of course, all your cousins. And we have front row seats so we can get a good view of the star!"

Zibby's mouth dropped. What was her mom doing, inviting the entire world? Too late, she realized what a mistake it had been not telling her parents she'd quit!

# CHAPTER 13

## ONE VERY LONG WEEK

The next morning Zibby woke up at six o'clock, unable to sleep any later, and padded downstairs in her slippers for her usual morning bowl of Cheerios. There, she found her dad, the early riser of the family, making oatmeal.

"Excited about the play?" her dad asked as he spooned brown sugar into his bowl.

Zibby swallowed extra hard. "Oh yeah, totally," she said in a small voice.

"Hmm," her father looked at her. "You don't sound too enthused."

"It's early," Zibby shrugged, pouring milk on her Cheerios and taking a big bite. They sat together companionably for a few minutes. Then Zibby asked, "Hey Dad, have you ever done something you know in your heart was right, but it ended up hurting a lot of people?"

"That's a big question for quarter past six in the morning," he said. "I'll have to think about that for a moment. Let me put on my thinking cap." He put a piece of the newspaper over his head and looked very serious, as if he were trying hard to make his brain work.

"Dad!" she said, smiling.

He took the newspaper off his head. "My answer is no. If you wind up hurting other people, what you're doing can't be right, no matter what your heart says."

"Oh," said Zibby, dropping her spoon into her Cheerios. This was one time in her life when her dad definitely *wasn't* going to make her feel better.

* * *

That week was maybe *the* worst in Zibby's whole life. Her friends ignored her on the blacktop before school, so she either stood alone or with her New And Very Irritating Best Friend, Franny Dewberry. At recess, since she wasn't wanted at the lunch tables or on the soccer field, she stayed inside and helped Miss Cannon grade papers or organize her bulletin boards.

During lunch, she gobbled down her sandwich in two minutes flat, then escaped to the library where no kids hung out except the Extreme Nerds, and they were too wrapped up in the "Math Olympiads" to care about the sixth-grade musical, much less Zibby's defection from it. Then after school, she returned to the library to wait out play rehearsal because she needed somewhere to go – she still hadn't told her parents she'd quit.

By Friday, Zibby was a wreck. The next day was the dress rehearsal, and she'd have to find somewhere to hide out for five hours while her parents thought she was rehearsing, but where would she go? And if the dress rehearsal was tomorrow, that meant there were only five more days until Opening Night, and with it, the unveiling of Zibby to her parents as a big fat fake and to her friends as a big fat quitter.

Sitting in the library at lunch, she sighed and gazed out the window, which overlooked the soccer field. *Well, well, well,* she thought, momentarily distracted from her mess of problems, *if it isn't a certain Ball Hog carrying a bright red hand-stitched, authentic pro leather ball with a built-in pump.* "There goes Shiloh again, trying to bully his way onto the field," Zibby said to herself.

But as she watched, Shiloh ran down the field and instead of taking the shot himself, passed the ball to Matthew. Matthew dribbled toward the goal a few feet, then shot and scored a goal. The two boys gave each other high fives, then ran back out to the field, laughing and talking.

*Look who has gone over to the good side,* thought Zibby, shaking her head in wonder.

* * *

Maybe it was a coincidence, or maybe fate, but the next morning, Saturday, she saw him again. She was at the market with her mom, trying not to let panic overtake her as the hours ticked closer to the dress rehearsal her parents were expecting her to attend, when she spied

Shiloh in the cereal aisle. At first, she was just going to ignore him, but then, despite her own woes, her curiosity caught up with her.

"So what happened?" she asked, planting herself by the "Sugar-Coated Chocolate Crunchies with Mini Marshmallows."

"Huh?" he grunted.

"Why'd you decide to let everyone play with your ball without all your special conditions?" she asked.

"I dunno," said Shiloh, shrugging. "I guess I got tired."

"Tired of what?" she asked.

"Everyone hating me and accusing me of wrecking the games," he said, looking up at her and meeting her eyes for the first time.

"Oh," she said.

"Could you move?" he asked. "You're blocking the 'Chocolate Crunchies.'"

"Oh," she said again, looking behind her. "No problem," she said as she stepped aside. "Well, see you around." She went to find her mom.

*Huh,* she thought. *So Shiloh had finally figured out soccer wasn't a solo sport.* If he'd only listened to her earlier, he would have saved himself some grief. Because if there was one thing she understood, it was soccer. She knew the rules, how to work as a team, when to pass, and when to score. She was a natural!

Compared to a play, soccer was easy. *If only sixth-*

*grade musicals were more like soccer*, she wished.

And just then Zibby was struck by a Revolutionary Thought. A thought that actually might make her stop being Public Enemy Number One and even more, might make her be able to finally do that stupid thing on page 83: Maybe the musical *was* like soccer after all!

And just like that, she knew what she had to do. She only hoped she wasn't too late.

# CHAPTER 14

## THE SHOW MUST GO ON

Once home from the market, Zibby plotted her next move. It was eleven o'clock in the morning; the dress rehearsal was in two hours. Her plan: Show up, apologize, ask to get the role of Miranda back, then pull off the Greatest Dress Rehearsal Mrs. Halpin had ever seen.

But first, she wanted to tell Sarah about her Big Revelation. She hoped that Sarah wouldn't be mad at her anymore and that they could get back to being best friends.

She dialed Sarah's cell and when Sarah answered, she yelled into the phone, "I've figure it out!"

"Zibby?" Sarah asked. "Figured what out?"

"How I can do page 83! If I just think about it like a pass to Matthew on the soccer field instead of a ... kiss, then maybe I can do it."

"Huh?" said Sarah.

"I know I've let down my team – you and Matthew and Camille and Mrs. Halpin and my parents and everyone in the play, but now I'm ready to pass the ball and get this game going! It's time for me to lace up my soccer shoes, get out there, and play!"

"I have no idea what you're talking about," Sarah said, sounding confused. "But if you're saying you want your role back, you'd better hurry over to the auditorium. Mrs. Halpin switched the dress rehearsal from one o'clock this afternoon to eight o'clock this morning, so we're almost finished!"

"Oh no!" Zibby gasped, hanging up the phone and flying out the front door.

\* \* \*

When Zibby arrived at the auditorium, the cast members were taking their curtain calls.

"Shoot!" she said to herself. *I've missed the entire rehearsal! And from the looks of everyone, it didn't go too well.*

Instead of looking pumped up after giving a great performance, almost everyone looked angry and tired.

Kids began to troop off stage, shooting Zibby dirty looks as they passed her.

"This play stinks," said Zane, glaring at her.

"I don't even want to invite my family," sniffed Camille.

Sarah walked by quickly, but didn't say anything to Zibby. She looked as if she'd been crying. And Matthew jumped down off the stage and retreated to the back of the auditorium.

The only person who seemed happy was Amber.

When she saw Zibby, she grabbed her wrist and squealed, "Did you see me up there?" she asked. "I stole the show. Mrs. Halpin said my 'Ouch' was a dramatic highlight she'll never forget."

"With such an unforgettable line, I don't doubt it," said Zibby.

She unlatched Amber's hand from her wrist and asked, "Do you know where Mrs. Halpin is?"

"Back there, somewhere," she motioned to the stage, then flitted over to Franny Dewberry, who was all smiles and appeared to be the Only Other Happy Person In The Room.

Backstage, Zibby found Mrs. Halpin putting a soccer ball and some other props in a box. She hadn't seen Mrs. Halpin since she'd quit the play and she was worried she might really let her have it, but Mrs. Halpin simply looked at her, and said, "Why, hello, dear."

"Um, so, how did the dress rehearsal go?" asked Zibby.

"Rocky to say the least," said Mrs. Halpin, her lips pursed. "Sarah tried her best, but she forgot half her lines, and that poor little Franny Dewberry is lost."

"Well," said Zibby, fidgeting with the hem of her T-shirt. "I might have a solution."

"Hmm," Mrs. Halpin murmured.

"I could take back my role as Miranda!" Zibby cried out. "I'm sorry for everything, and I'm ready to do that thing ... um, the kiss ... now," she said, correcting herself.

Mrs. Halpin gave her an icy stare. "You mean, five days before the performance, after skipping the last week of rehearsal *and* the dress rehearsal and after throwing the entire production into chaos, you want to come back as Miranda?" she asked frostily.

"Yes," said Zibby.

"Let Sarah go back to being Deirdre, Camille back to being the principal, and send poor little Franny Dewberry back to the chorus?"

"Yes!"

"Kiss Matthew in the final scene with no hesitations, fake colds, fake lips or any other excuses?"

"Yes," repeated Zibby. "I can do it!"

"That's a lot to ask after what you've put us through," said Mrs. Halpin.

"I know," said Zibby, hanging her head.

"And I will have to say ..." Mrs. Halpin's voice trailed off.

Zibby waited, biting her lip.

"Bless you, my dear. Yes! This solves all the problems! This musical may have a chance yet!"

She grabbed Zibby by the hand and dragged her out to the center of the stage. Clapping her hands, she yelled, "Students! I'm here to announce that Zibby has reconsidered and will be stepping back into the role of Miranda, which means you will all return to your original roles."

Everyone started cheering excitedly. Zibby was

relieved to look down and see Sarah giving her the thumbs up and smiling, and Camille clapping. In fact, all the kids looked thrilled about Mrs. Halpin's announcement, except for Franny Dewberry, who burst into tears and ran out of the auditorium.

The next thing Zibby knew, Sarah had run up on stage and was standing by her side. "Thank you," she said as she threw her arms around Zibby. "I was gonna totally mess up the role of Miranda."

"I'm so sorry for what I did," said Zibby. "I feel terrible!"

"And I'm sorry I've been so mean to you lately," said Sarah.

They would have said more, but Zibby was crushed by other members of the cast who were surrounding her, welcoming her back – Camille, Amber, Zane, everyone but Matthew, who was conspicuously absent.

After Zibby disentangled herself from the crowd on the stage, she went looking for him. She found him in one of the back rows of the auditorium, stuffing his script into his backpack.

"Hi," she said.

"Hi," Matthew said, looking intently at his backpack.

"I just wanted to say ... I'm really sorry," said Zibby. "I hope I didn't hurt your feelings or anything. It wasn't anything personal; I was just really freaked out for a while."

Matthew looked at her. "It's okay," he said.

"Really? Because you're, like, my best guy friend, and if I lost you over this, I'd be so sad that I'd have to give up soccer or something!"

"Don't do that, tomboy!" he said, smiling.

"So it's okay between us?" she asked, feeling relieved.

"It's okay," he said. Then he added, "You know that, um, time on your front porch."

"Yes," she said guardedly.

"That was just for the show," he said. "Part of getting into character. It didn't mean anything – *that way*."

"Of course not!" said Zibby. "You were just preparing for the role."

They were quiet for a moment.

"Hey, you know what?" asked Zibby. "I think this is going to be the Very Best Musical Mrs. Halpin ever put on!"

"Me, too," said Matthew.

But before they could speculate any more about just how fabulous the play was going to be, Mrs. Halpin's voice boomed across the auditorium.

"Zibby dear, I hope you still remember all your lines."

Zibby gulped. *Right. My lines,* she thought. She hoped she remembered them too!

# CHAPTER 15

## OPENING NIGHT

On the first night of the performance, Zibby sat in the girls' dressing room studying her lines one more time.

Her stomach was churning and her mouth felt as dry as Scotch tape.

But it wasn't her lines that were troubling her. She still knew them by heart, and was just checking them again to be sure.

It was all page 83's fault! Again!

Who was she kidding? A kiss wasn't a soccer pass. It was a KISS! A boy-mouth meets girl-mouth lip lock!

She looked longingly at a stage door that lead outside. There was still time to slip out. To escape ...

"Your turn, dear," Mrs. Halpin's voice startled her. "Makeup time!" She held up a large black case and slammed it on the table in front of Zibby.

"Please, no!" protested Zibby.

"You must wear a little foundation," Mrs. Halpin said as she withdrew a small compact from the case and opened it up, revealing a thick, brown paste-like substance. "Otherwise you'll look yellow on stage." She applied what felt like slime all over Zibby's face.

"And *this* keeps the shine away," she said, whipping out a large puff and patting Zibby's nose with it.

"Hey," Zibby started coughing as she inhaled a toxic cloud of powder.

"No fake coughing, dear," said Mrs. Halpin.

"It's for real!" protested Zibby.

Ignoring her, Mrs. Halpin dabbed some blush and lipstick on Zibby, then moved in with a mascara wand.

"Not that!" Zibby wailed, shielding her eyes with her hands. "That thing looks like an instrument of death!"

"Settle down," said Mrs. Halpin, gripping Zibby's shoulder, and then lightly tipping her chin up. She swiftly glued Zibby's eyelashes together – or at least, that's how it felt to Zibby as she blinked, blinked again, and blinked one more time to clear her vision.

"There! You're done!" Mrs. Halpin said, moving on to Amber, who was sitting next to Zibby.

"Hey, Mrs. Halpin," Amber asked. "Can I use my own lip gloss?" She waved a tube of something called "New & Improved Groovy Grapilicious."

"I guess so," said Mrs. Halpin, applying foundation on Amber's face.

"Thank you!" squealed Amber. "This is a cool new type with advanced technology – it's called a volumizer. It adds one-eighth of an inch to the size of your lips so you look like Angelina Jolie."

"Hmm," murmured Mrs. Halpin absentmindedly, as she expertly zapped blush and mascara on Amber, then moved down to the next girl in line for makeup.

But Zibby was listening intently – and getting the beginnings of A Very Good Idea.

"So, that lip gloss actually makes your lips bigger?" she asked Amber.

"Yep, it's almost like having an extra set of lips," squealed Amber. "I *luuuvvv* it!" she said, and then put on another coat.

"Can I borrow that for the play?" asked Zibby.

"You told Mrs. Halpin you didn't want any more makeup," said Amber, narrowing her eyes. "Plus, you hate lip gloss!"

"But maybe I need Angelina Jolie lips for the play, too," said Zibby.

"Well, okay. I guess so," said Amber, handing the tube to Zibby. "Besides, it's not like it's my only one." She opened a pink makeup bag with her name spelled out in rhinestones that was lying on her lap to reveal many more tubes.

"Thanks," said Zibby, cramming the lip gloss into her soccer sock, and giving it a little pat. Groovy Grapilicious lip gloss had gotten her into this kiss, and now it just might be her ticket out.

* * *

Standing in the wings, waiting for the final scene, Zibby reached into her sock and pulled out the lip gloss.

She put on one coat, then another, then a third, then a fourth. By now, her lips were tingling and feeling like a sticky mess. What's worse, she smelled like a crate-load of spilled grape soda. But it was worth it.

*This way, Matthew won't really be kissing me, he'll be kissing my lip gloss – all one-half inch of it,* she thought to herself. *They're so chemically enhanced, Matthew won't be able to find my real lips no matter how hard he tries!*

Just then Mrs. Halpin appeared from backstage. "You're on in ..." she checked her watch ... "exactly eight seconds."

"I'm ready," said Zibby.

"Good," said Mrs. Halpin. "And I'm counting, five, four, three, two, one, now!"

Zibby just stood there.

"You're on!" repeated Mrs. Halpin.

Zibby didn't move.

"Go!" said Mrs. Halpin, and she shoved Zibby out onto the stage.

Suddenly, Zibby found herself standing in the middle of the pep rally scene, with all eyes on her.

"Thank you all for your support," she said, launching into her line. "Winning the championship has been the biggest highlight of my life, and winning it for the school makes the victory even sweeter."

"And I'd like to present you with the Most Valuable Player trophy," boomed Matthew in a loud stage voice.

"Thank you so much," said Zibby, trying to override

her own personal frown of fear with Miranda's smile of joy, but ending up with more of a grimace than a grin.

"And I'd also like to present you with this," said Matthew. He leaned close to Zibby, then moved closer, lips puckered, when ... he stopped suddenly.

"What's with your lips?" he whispered in horror.

"They're *volumized*," she whispered back.

He gave a little frown, puckered his lips again, and moved toward her lips when at the last second, he ducked out of the kiss and grazed Zibby's chin instead.

"I can't kiss those greasy lips!" he cried out.

Zibby was furious! Insulted!

"Oh no you don't," she said, grabbing his shirt collar with both hands and pulling him toward her. "After all I've been through, you're not wimping out on me now!"

And she laid a Big One on him, sliming him in "New & Improved Groovy Grapilicious" lip gloss!

When she was finished, she let go of Matthew so quickly and so suddenly that he fell over backward and went tumbling onto the floor. But Zibby didn't notice. She clasped her hands over her head in victory, turned to the audience and yelled, "*I did it!*"

The audience began to clap. And clap some more. And soon the auditorium reverberated with the sound of 600 pairs of hands.

Someone threw a bouquet of roses onto the stage, and Zibby reached down to pick it up, then bowed deeply to her adoring fans.

She looked at the crowd and picked out her mom, her face all scrunched up as if she were half-crying, half-laughing. And there was Anthony, giving her a thumbs up, and her cousins, waving to her as if she were a movie star, and her dad ... oddly, frantically pointing at something on the stage.

She looked around, perplexed, and then finally saw Matthew, who was still sitting on the floor looking dazed.

"Get up!" Zibby cried. "Take a bow – they love us!"

But Matthew didn't move.

"Hey tomboy," he called up to her, giving her a wide grin. "That was some kiss. I can't wait until the show tomorrow night ... and the next."

"*Whaaat?*" Zibby exclaimed.

Her face fell.

And *bam*! So did the curtain.

## THE END

# Also available from the "Zibby Payne" series:

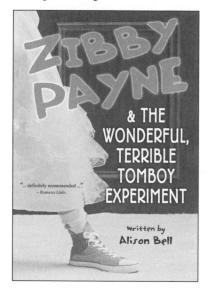

## Zibby Payne & the Wonderful, Terrible Tomboy Experiment
### by Alison Bell
**ISBN: 978-1-897073-39-1**

It's the first day of school, and Zibby Payne can't believe how much her friends have changed ... for the worse! At recess, all they want to do is put on makeup, fix their hair, and talk about boys – *ugh*!

Zibby decides there's only one way to save the school year – she'll become a total tomboy. She dumps her frilly outfits, starts playing soccer with the boys, and learns to do some awesome new things, like belch out the alphabet. Even if her old friends are giving her dirty looks, Zibby's having the time of her life ... until she tries to form an exclusive "Tomboy Club" and her experiment starts to backfire.

Can Zibby find a way to be different and still keep her best friend, or will she end up one lonely, unhappy tomboy?

**www.lobsterpress.com**